D0191725

Quentin Blake

COCKATOOS

RED FOX

to my friends in France

Other books by Quentin Blake:

ALL JOIN IN
ANGEL PAVEMENT
CLOWN
FANTASTIC DAISY ARTICHOKE
THE GREEN SHIP
LOVEYKINS
MISTER MAGNOLIA
MRS ARMITAGE AND THE BIG WAVE
MRS ARMITAGE ON WHEELS
MRS ARMITAGE QUEEN OF THE ROAD
QUENTIN BLAKE'S ABC
A SAILING BOAT IN THE SKY
SIMPKIN
ZAGAZOO

COCKATOOS
A RED FOX BOOK 978 0 099 96490 2

First published in Great Britain by Jonathan Cape,
an imprint of Random House Children's Publishers UK
A Random House Group Company

Jonathan Cape edition published 1992
Red Fox edition published 1994

25 26 27 28 29 30

Red Fox Books are published by Random House Children's Publishers UK
61–63 Uxbridge Road, London W5 5SA

www.randomhousechildrens.co.uk

Addresses for companies within The Random House Group Limited can be found at:
www.randomhouse.co.uk/offices.htm

THE RANDOM HOUSE GROUP Limited Reg. No. 954009

A CIP catalogue record for this book is available from the British Library.

Printed in China

Professor Dupont had ten cockatoos.
He was very proud of them.

Every morning he jumped out of bed.

He took a shower and
    he cleaned his teeth,

    as he always did.

He got dressed and he tied his tie,
as he always did.

He adjusted his spectacles,
as he always did.

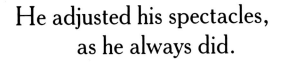

And he went downstairs.

He went into the conservatory.
There were all his cockatoos;
　　　　　　every single one.

Professor Dupont threw wide his arms.
He said: "Good morning,
　　　　　my fine feathered friends!"

Every morning he said the same thing.
The day came when the cockatoos thought they would go
mad if they had to listen to the same words once again.

They decided to have some sport with Professor Dupont.
One after another they escaped through a broken pane of
glass they had discovered in a corner of the conservatory.

Next morning Professor Dupont came into the
conservatory and threw wide his arms.
There was not a cockatoo in sight.

Where could all the cockatoos have got to?

Professor Dupont went into the dining-room.
They weren't there.

He went to look in the kitchen.
Hortense the cook was there,
boiling an egg for his breakfast,
but there weren't any cockatoos.

He went to look in the bedroom.
They weren't there.

He looked in the bathroom.
They weren't there.

He looked in the lavatory.
They weren't there.

He climbed a ladder
and flashed his torch around the attic.
They weren't there.

He even climbed up to the roof.
But they weren't there.

Professor Dupont went to look in the garage.
His car was there,
but there weren't any cockatoos.

He went down into the cellar; but he couldn't see
any cockatoos there, either.

Professor Dupont was at his wits' end.
He couldn't find his cockatoos anywhere.
Where could they possibly have got to?

Professor Dupont spent a restless night.

The next morning he jumped out of bed.
He took a shower and he cleaned his teeth,
as he always did.

He got dressed and he tied his tie,
as he always did.

He adjusted his spectacles,
as he always did.

And he went downstairs.

Professor Dupont went into the conservatory.
There were all his cockatoos, where they
always were – every single one!

Professor Dupont threw wide his arms.
He said: "Good morning,
my fine feathered friends!"

Some people never learn.